D1228156

MIMI'S STRATEGY

What to do when your sister takes your toys

Written by
Linda Goudsmit

Illustrated by
Xavier Pom

Published by Waldorf Publishing
2140 Hall Johnson Road
#102-345
Grapevine, Texas 76051
www.WaldorfPublishing.com

Mimi's Strategy:
What to do when your sister takes your toys

ISBN: 9781643165790
Library of Congress Control Number: 2018943862

Illustrations by Xavier Pom
Design by Baris Celik

To my darling granddaughter Beatrice
who inspired Mimi's Strategies - with
forever love from her Mimi

Once upon a time there was a little girl named Hildy who lived in the country with her Mama, her Papa, and her little sister Francesca.

Hildy loved Francesca and Hildy loved being Francesca's big sister,
but SOMETIMES Hildy got into trouble!!

I will tell you why.

Francesca loved Hildy and wanted to be just like Hildy.

Francesca wanted to do whatever Hildy did.

Francesca wanted to go wherever Hildy went.

Francesca wanted to say whatever Hildy said.

Francesca wanted to sing whatever Hildy sang.

.....and wanted to read whatever Hildy read.

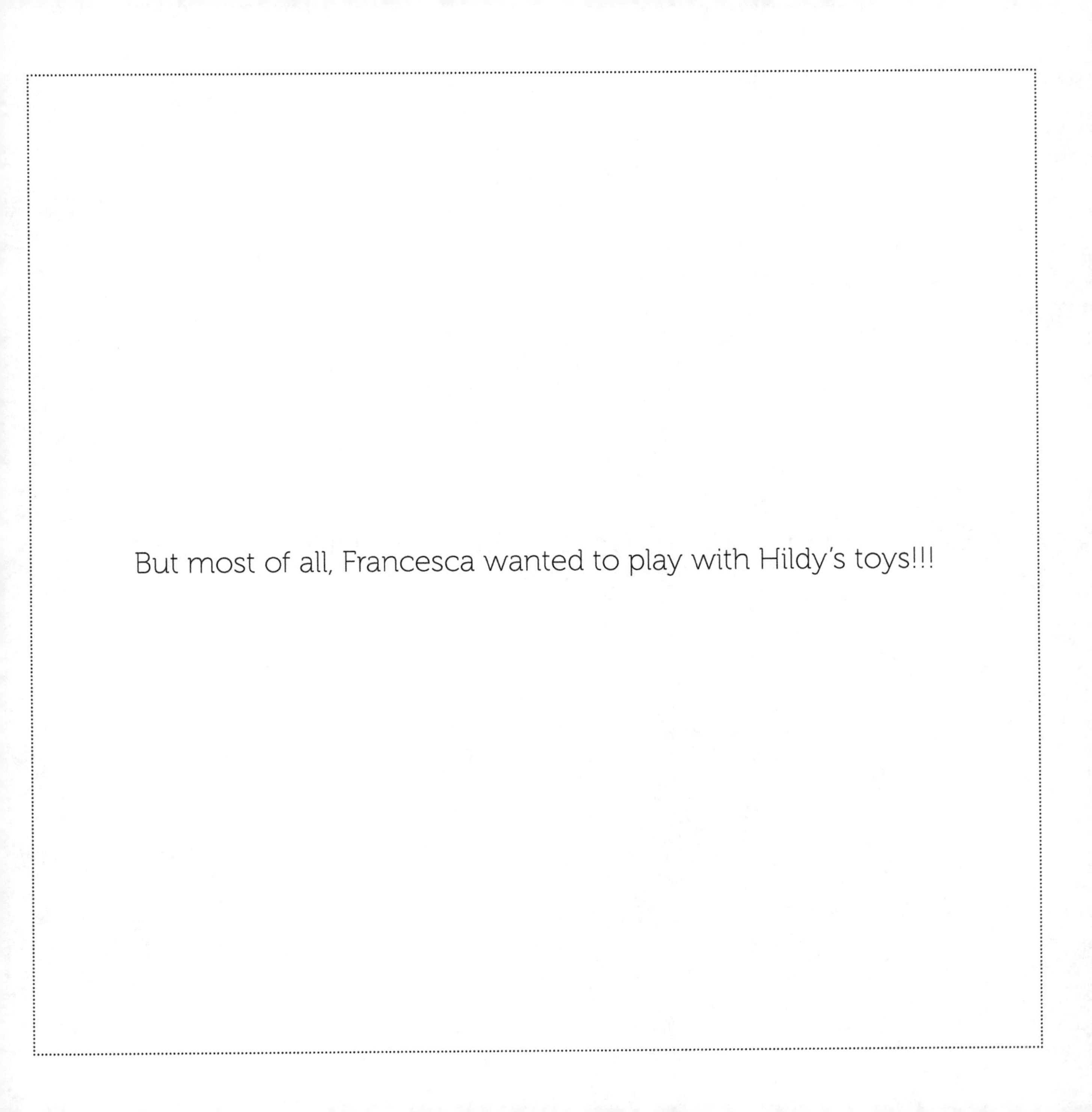

But most of all, Francesca wanted to play with Hildy's toys!!!

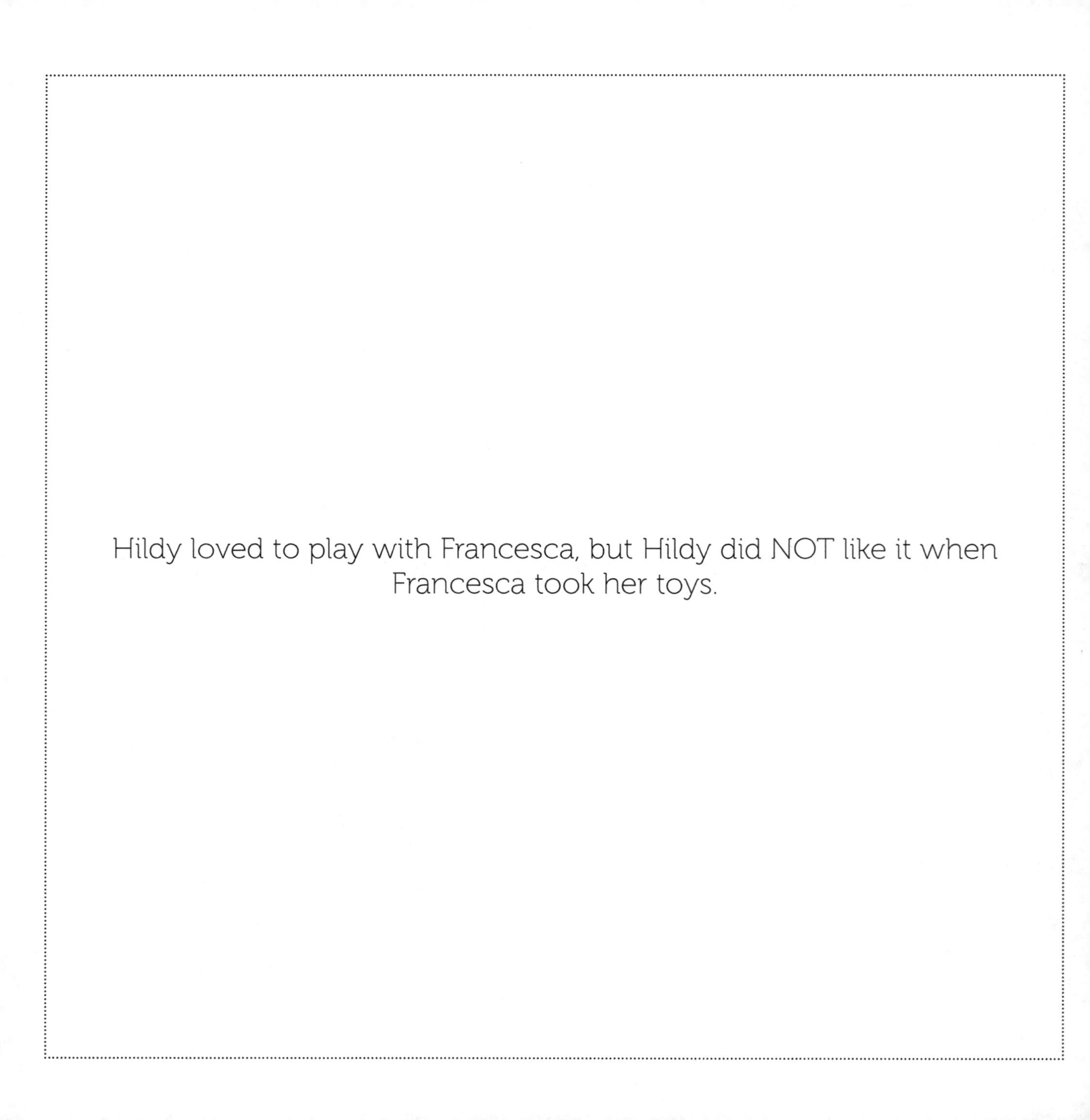

Hildy loved to play with Francesca, but Hildy did NOT like it when Francesca took her toys.

What was Hildy supposed to do?

First, Hildy tried grabbing her toy back.

"WHAAAA!!!" Francesca started wailing!!

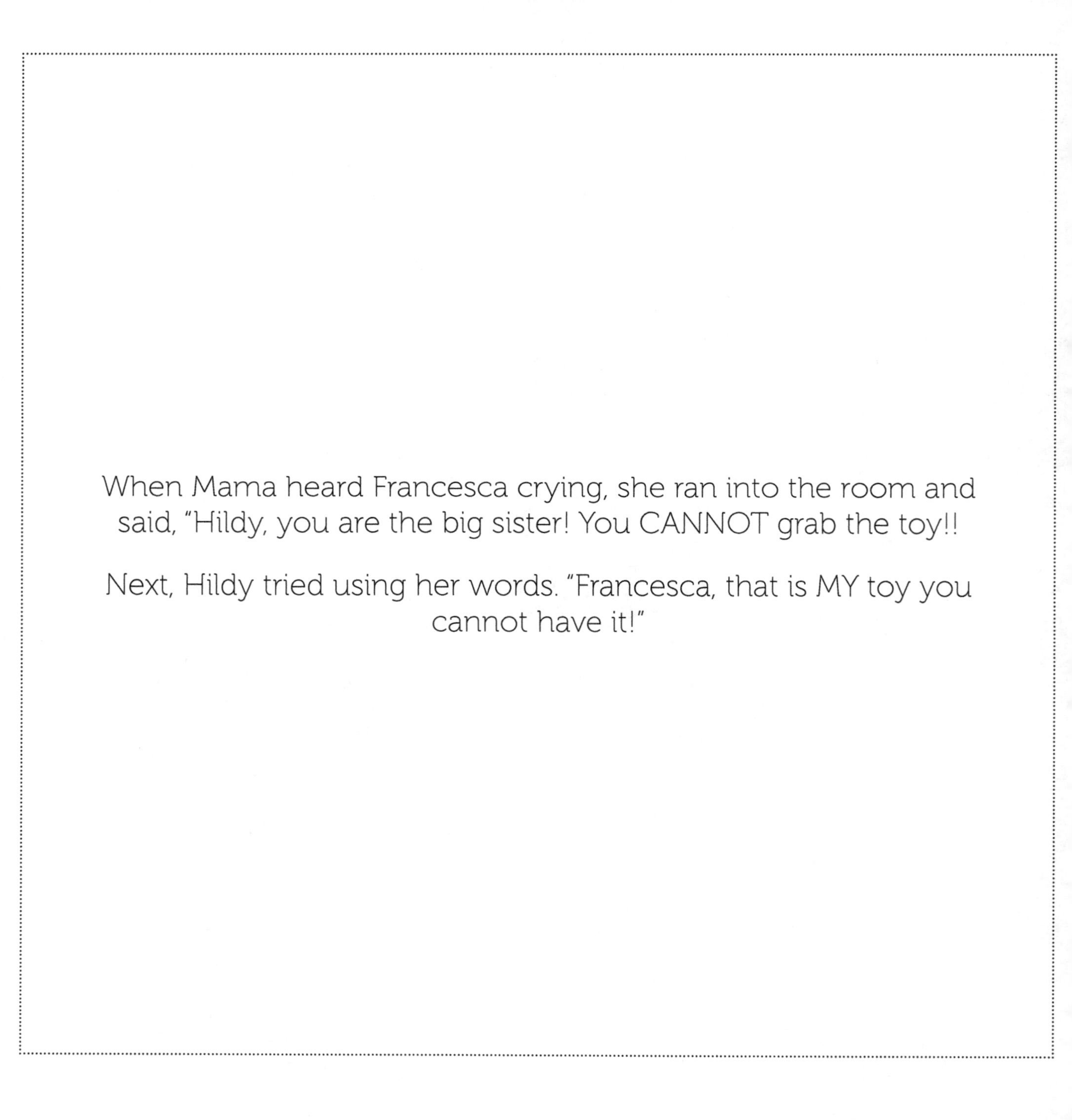

When Mama heard Francesca crying, she ran into the room and said, "Hildy, you are the big sister! You CANNOT grab the toy!!

Next, Hildy tried using her words. "Francesca, that is MY toy you cannot have it!"

"WHAAAA!!!" Francesca started wailing again.

When Mama heard Francesca crying again, she ran into the room and said, "Hildy, you are the big sister! You have to share!!"

Next, Hildy tried taking turns.

"WHAAAA!!!" Francesca just kept on screaming, "MINE! MINE! MINE!"

When Mama heard Francesca screaming, she ran into the room and said, “Hildy, now you are going into time out!”

Being in time out made Hildy VERY sad and VERY angry. It seemed that no matter how hard Hildy tried, she could not get it right.

THEN, Hildy remembered Mimi's STRATEGY!!!

Mimi and Zeze were Hildy's grandparents who lived far, far away in Florida. When Mimi came to visit she said to Hildy, "Hildy, you need a STRATEGY!"

"What is a strategy Mimi?"

"A strategy is a plan darling."

"What is my plan Mimi?"

"You love your sister, right?"

"Right Mimi."

"When you play with your sister, she takes your toys, right?"

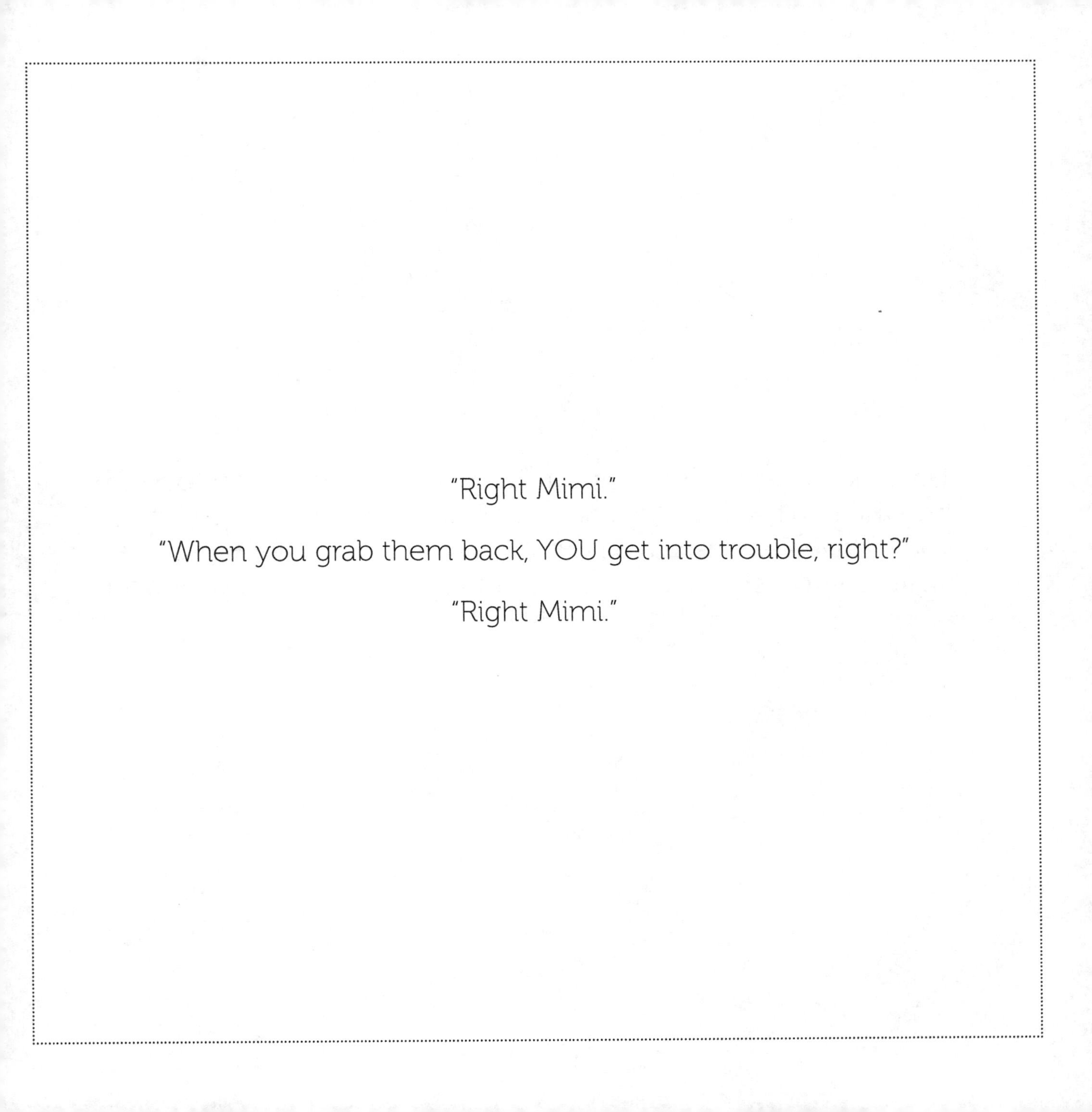

"Right Mimi."

"When you grab them back, YOU get into trouble, right?"

"Right Mimi."

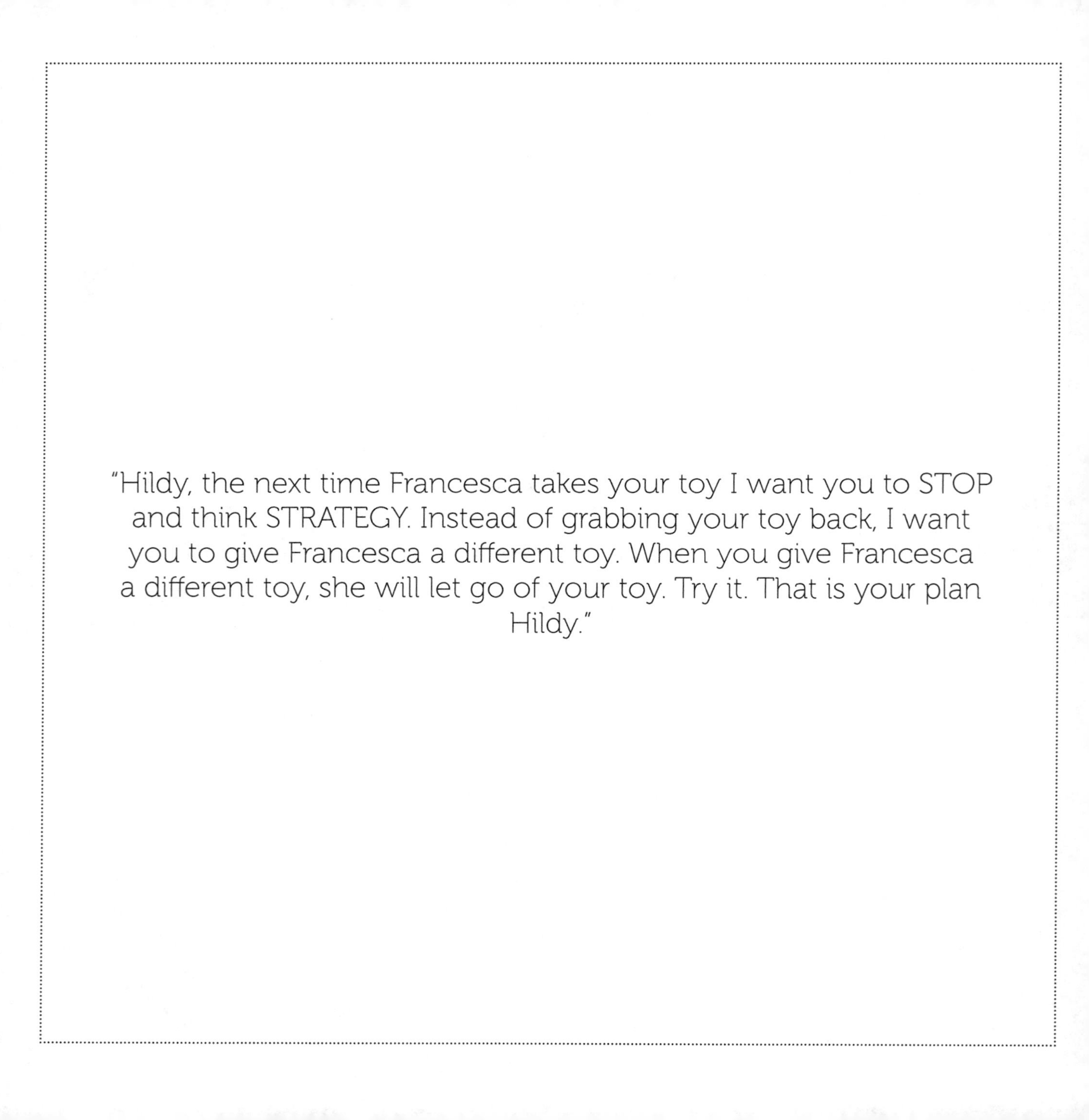

"Hildy, the next time Francesca takes your toy I want you to STOP and think STRATEGY. Instead of grabbing your toy back, I want you to give Francesca a different toy. When you give Francesca a different toy, she will let go of your toy. Try it. That is your plan Hildy."

The very next day, Hildy and Francesca were playing with their toys.

Hildy had her bunny, and Francesca had her frog.

Suddenly, Francesca reached out and took Hildy's bunny.

"MINE! MINE! MINE!"

Just as Hildy was about to grab her bunny back, she STOPPED and remembered Mimi's STRATEGY!

Hildy looked to her right, and Hildy looked to her left and then Hildy saw Francesca's ducky.

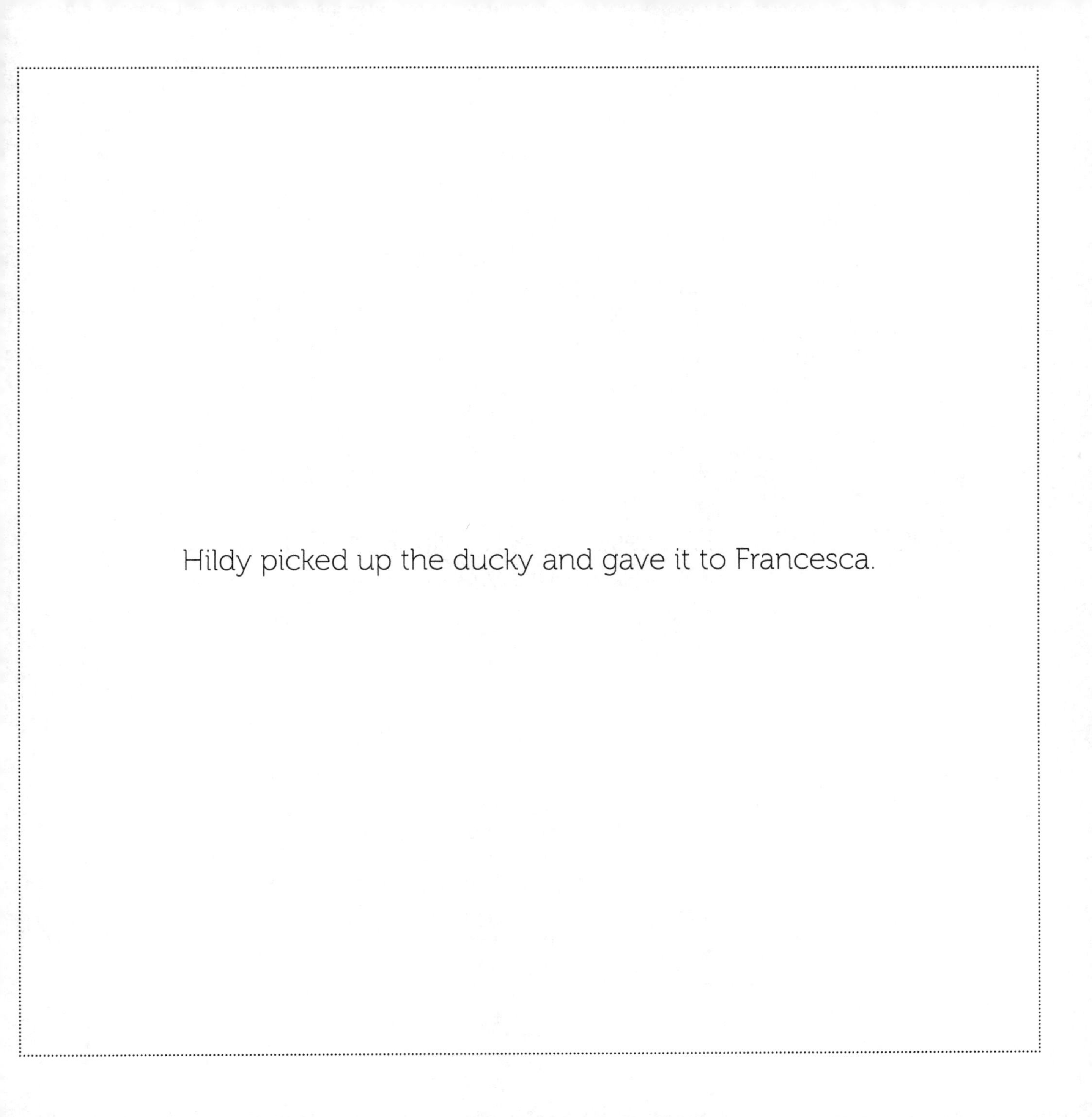

Hildy picked up the ducky and gave it to Francesca.

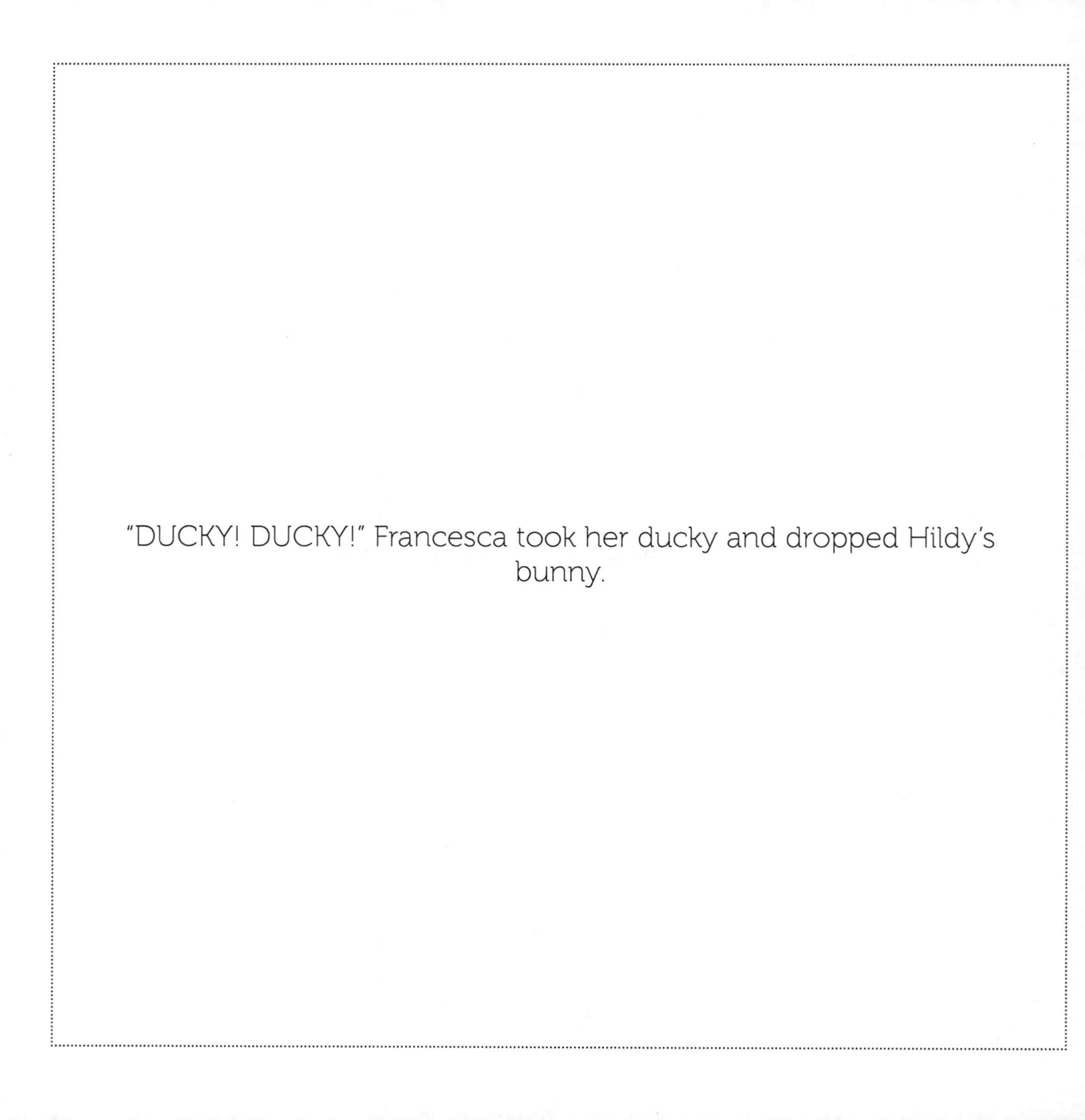

"DUCKY! DUCKY!" Francesca took her ducky and dropped Hildy's bunny.

When Mama heard all the commotion, she ran into the room
and hugged and kissed Hildy, "You are such a wonderful big sister
Hildy! I am very very proud of you!"

Hildy was SO happy!

When Hildy used her new STRATEGY, she got her toy back, she did not get into trouble, and her Mama was very proud of her!

So if your little sister takes your toys, and you end up in trouble, I think you should try Mimi's STRATEGY too.

THE END

Linda Goudsmit is a devoted wife to husband Rob and they are the parents of four children and the grandparents of four. She and Rob owned and operated a girls clothing store in Michigan for forty years before retiring to the sunny beaches of Florida. A graduate of the University of Michigan in Ann Arbor, Linda has a lifelong commitment to learning and is an avid reader and observer of life. She is the author of the philosophy book *Dear America: Who's Driving the Bus?* and numerous current affairs articles featured on her website www.lindagoudsmit.com

CPSIA information can be obtained
at www.ICGtesting.com
Printed in the USA
BVHW011959131019
560927BV00001B/3/P

9 781643 165790